what is happening in the pictures.

Each child is an individual and develops at his own pace. Be patient if your child is struggling with words. It is more important to value what he *can* do than to become anxious about progress. The learning steps will all be taken in time, with your help. At the back of this book you will find suggestions on how to make the best and fullest use of **Talkabout starting school**.

* In order to avoid the clumsy 'he/she', the child is referred to as 'he'.

Geraldine Taylor is a national broadcaster, writer and authority on involving parents in their children's education. She contributes on this subject regularly to magazines for parents.

Working with schools in Avon, Geraldine helps parents and teachers to act in partnership to benefit children's learning confidence and family happiness.

Acknowledgments
The publishers would like to thank Bramford Primary School, Bramford, Ipswich, Suffolk, and Patricia Chubb, Headteacher, Ashley Down Infants' School, Bristol, for their help.

British Library Cataloguing in Publication Data

Taylor, Geraldine
    Talkabout starting school.
    1. English language—Readers—For pre school children
    I. Title   II. Breeze, Lynn   III. Series
    428.6
    ISBN 0-7214-1086-3

Published by Ladybird Books Ltd Loughborough Leicestershire UK
Ladybird Books Inc Auburn Maine 04210 USA

Printed in England

talkabout
starting school

written by GERALDINE TAYLOR
illustrated by LYNN BREEZE

Ladybird Books

Your teacher will welcome you.

You will soon have lots of new friends.

You will have your own drawer and
your own bag for your things.

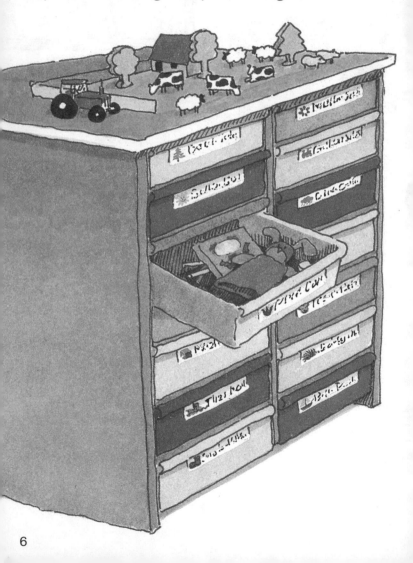

What will be inside *your* bag?

You will have your own peg
for your coat.

You can go to the toilet

...and you can wash your hands,
just as you do at home.

You can paint and make models.

What would you like to do?

There are lots of lovely books
to look at and to read.

Which books do you like?

Sometimes a computer will help you to learn.

Everyone goes out to play.

Here are some of the people who will help you at school.

Sometimes mums and dads come in
to help, too.

Everyone comes to assembly to talk
and sing about the world we live in.

You will learn how to read
and write words.

21

You will sort and weigh things

...and you will measure and count.

Many children have dinner at school.

Some children bring a packed lunch to eat instead.

Perhaps you will all go on a visit.

There may be concerts and plays for parents and friends to see.

And there will be other times
when mums, dads and friends
will come to your school.

There may be animals at school
to care for...

We are growing cress and some bulbs.

...and perhaps you will grow plants.

Sometimes you will cook.

Mmm... something smells good!

P.E. is very exciting.
You will run and jump.

You will listen to stories.

Sometimes you will be able to tell stories, too.

Which of these stories can you
tell now?

There will be time to sing
and make music.

Can you sing these rhymes?

Twinkle, twinkle, little star,
How I wonder what you are!
Up above the world so high,
Like a diamond in the sky...

*   *   *

Hickory, dickory, dock,
The mouse ran up the clock.
The clock struck one,
The mouse ran down,
Hickory, dickory, dock.

Time to go home!

There will be such a lot to talk about.

starting school

The text and illustrations in **talkabout starting school** are carefully planned to encourage children to talk about the experiences they will meet at school.

Starting school is such a big step towards independence that naturally most children feel apprehensive as well as excited. Headteachers understand this and will usually invite parents and children to visit the school before the start of the first term.

During these visits children and parents can make friends with their teacher. They can see what the school buildings are like, and see some of the activities inside and sometimes outside, too. Before and after this visit, though, children will want to talk about what they will *do* at school.

Talkabout starting school will help you and your child to explore these new experiences. Children will be reassured by talking about where their belongings will go and by